THE
LION KING

This is the story of an adventuresome lion cub,
who must find his own place in the great Circle of Life.

As the morning sun rose high over the African plain, animals and birds gathered at the foot of Pride Rock. This was a very special day!

The animals bowed when they saw the new prince, Simba, before them.

King Mufasa and Queen Sarabi watched as Rafiki, the wise baboon, presented their newborn son to the kingdom.

Simba grew into a playful and curious cub. Early one morning, Mufasa brought Simba to the top of Pride Rock.

"Everything the light touches is our kingdom," he told his son. "One day, Simba, the sun will set on my time here, and will rise with you as the new king. We are all connected in the great Circle of Life."

Later that day, Simba went to see his Uncle Scar.

"My dad just showed me the whole kingdom," the cub bragged. "And I'm gonna rule it all!"

Now, Scar was angry that he was no longer next in line to be king. He was plotting to get rid of this new prince. He asked slyly if Mufasa had shown him what was beyond the northern border.

"Well, no," said Simba sadly. "He said I can't go there."

"And he's absolutely right," said Scar. "Far too dangerous. Only the bravest lions go there. An elephant graveyard is no place for a young prince."

Simba didn't see his uncle's evil trap. He decided to show his father what a brave cub he could be.

Simba set out to find his best friend, Nala—and go visit the elephant graveyard that very day. He had no idea that Scar had ordered three hyenas to go to the elephant graveyard, too—to kill the new prince!

Simba raced ahead across the plains, leading Nala to the forbidden place. Eventually they reached a pile of bones.

"It's really creepy," said Nala.

Simba was about to explore a skull when he saw Zazu, his father's trusted adviser.

Zazu commanded them to leave immediately, saying, "We are all in very real danger!"

But it was already too late! Nala and Simba were trapped by three laughing, drooling hyenas!

Simba took a deep breath and tried to roar—but only a squeaky rumble came out. The hyenas laughed even more at that.

Simba took another deep breath.

"*ROAARR!*"

The three hyenas looked around into the eyes of...

…King Mufasa!

His giant paw struck one of the hyenas
as he growled, "If you ever come near
my son again…"

The hyenas fled howling into the
mist before he could finish.

Mufasa scolded his son on the way home. "You deliberately disobeyed me."

"I was just trying to be brave, like you," said Simba softly.

"Being brave doesn't mean you go looking for trouble," replied Mufasa.

The moon shone brightly above them and the stars twinkled in the dark sky.

Mufasa stopped. "Look at the stars! The great kings of the past look down on us from those stars. So, whenever you feel alone, just remember that those kings will always be there to guide you, and so will I."

Meanwhile, Scar came up with another plan to get rid of King Mufasa and Simba. Scar led Simba down a steep gorge. Then Scar signaled the hyenas to frighten a herd of wildebeests. The wildebeests stampeded toward Simba!

Hearing the thunder of hooves, Mufasa raced to the rescue!

"Hold on, Simba!" he cried.

The king rescued his son, but he could not save himself, for Scar pushed him into the stampede of wildebeests!

When the stampede was over, Simba ran to his father's side.

"Dad," he whimpered, nuzzling Mufasa's mane.

But the king did not reply, and Simba started sobbing.

"Simba," said Scar coldly, "what have you done? The king is dead, and if it weren't for you, he'd still be alive. What will your mother think? Run away, Simba. Run away and never return."

Heartbroken, poor Simba ran away as fast as he could.

Scar was certain that Simba would never come back. He returned to take the royal throne at Pride Rock for himself.

Meanwhile, Simba was far away from the Pride Lands. The ground turned dry and cracked beneath him. The hot sun beat down as vultures circled above his head.

Exhausted and unable to go any farther, Simba slumped to the ground.

After a long while, Simba awoke. Everything around him looked different. There were trees and grass and flowers instead of desert. A meerkat named Timon and a warthog named Pumbaa had brought him to their home.

"You nearly died," said Pumbaa.

"I saved you!" added Timon. "Well, uh, Pumbaa helped."

"Thanks for your help," said Simba; but he thought, *It doesn't matter. I've got nowhere to go.* He began to walk away.

"Where ya going?" asked Timon kindly.

"Nowhere," said Simba.

"Anything we can do?" said Pumbaa.

"Not unless you can change the past."

"You gotta put your past behind ya," said
Timon. "Repeat after me: *Hakuna matata!*"

"It means: No worries," added Pumbaa.

Simba decided to stay in the jungle with
his new friends.

Years passed and Simba grew into a young lion. He lived
a happy, carefree, no-worries life with his friends.

But one day something happened that was *not* a
no-worries situation! A fierce lioness was about to
spring onto Pumbaa, who was stuck under a tree root!

"She's gonna eat me!" squealed Pumbaa.

Simba rushed over to help.

Simba wrestled with the lioness, but then realized she was his old friend Nala. "You're alive!" she said happily. "That means you're the king!"

Nala told Simba how Scar had destroyed the Pride Lands. "Simba, if you don't do something, soon everyone will starve."

"I can't go back. You wouldn't understand," said Simba.

Nala was disappointed in her friend. "*Don't* you understand? You're our only hope."

Nala turned and left her friend alone.

That night, Simba lay by a stream, thinking. He heard a noise and looked up. It was Rafiki.

"I know who you are," said Rafiki. "You're Mufasa's boy. He's alive, and I'll show him to you. You follow Rafiki. Come on."

Simba followed Rafiki in wonder to the edge of the stream. As Simba looked into the water, his reflection changed shape and became his father's! He heard Mufasa's voice from the stars.

"Simba. Remember who you are. You are my son and the one true king."

Then the reflection and Rafiki disappeared.

"I am going back," decided Simba.

Meanwhile, back at the Pride Lands, storm
clouds had gathered and a lightning bolt scorched
the earth. As the dry grasses caught fire, huge
flames swept toward Pride Rock—and a lion
appeared through the smoke.

It was Simba!

Scar lunged at Simba, determined to kill him just as he had Mufasa. Timon and Pumbaa joined in the fierce battle that followed, as the lionesses drove back the hyenas. Simba finally heaved Scar over a cliff. Scar landed—to find himself surrounded by drooling hyenas.

Simba was victorious!

Simba took his rightful place as the Lion King, and once again the land flourished.

One dawn, the animals and birds made their way again to the foot of Pride Rock. Rafiki picked up a tiny cub. He showed the new princess—the daughter of King Simba and Queen Nala—to the cheering crowd below.

The Circle of Life would continue.